The Moon Is Beautiful, Isn't It?

Ansh Tanwar

Published by Sellbrochure Vymish Entertainment, 2024.

THE MOON IS BEAUTIFUL, ISN'T IT?

First edition. July 31, 2024.

Copyright © 2024 Ansh Tanwar.

ISBN: 979-8227967671

Written by Ansh Tanwar.

Hey Greetings,

Holding this book in your hand, sinking back in your soft arm- chair, you will say to yourself: perhaps it will amuse me. And after you have read this story of great misfortunes, you will no doubt dine well, blaming the author for your own insensitivity, accusing him of wild exaggeration and flights of fancy. But rest assured: "I leave it upto you to decide whether this is a tragedy of fiction or reality,but imagine it as a romantic tale."

Honoré de Balzac, Le Père Goriot

Author:- Ansh Tanwar

Introduction:- Aryan

Aryan was the quintessential middle-class boy, his life marked by a series of struggles and small victories that shaped his character before he even stepped into college. Growing up, he navigated the challenges of a modest upbringing with resilience and determination, each hardship fueling his hope for a better future. The dreams of a new chapter, filled with good friends and enriching experiences, kept him going.

Music was Aryan's true passion. He had a natural talent for singing and aspired to be a musician, often losing himself in melodies and lyrics that spoke to his soul. However, life had other plans, and fate led him to medical school. Despite this unexpected turn, Aryan remained hopeful, his eyes gleaming with the possibility of honing new skills and discovering latent talents. He approached his studies with the same dedication he had for music, finding parallels in the discipline and creativity required for both fields.

Family was the cornerstone of Aryan's life. He deeply loved his parents and cherished every moment spent with them. But it was his brother who held the most special place in his heart. Their bond was unbreakable, forged through shared dreams, mutual support, and countless late-night conversations about life and aspirations. Aryan's love for his brother was a driving force, inspiring him to strive for success and happiness.

Aryan was a unique blend of introvert and extrovert. He could be reserved and introspective, thriving in quiet moments of reflection, yet he could also be outgoing and sociable, seamlessly fitting into lively gatherings. This duality made him adaptable and approachable, a friend to many and a confidant to a few. He understood people, sensing when to listen and when to speak, a trait that made his relationships genuine and deep.

A hopeless romantic at heart, Aryan believed in the beauty of true love. He yearned for a special someone, a person he could commit to for a lifetime. His ideals were old-fashioned in the best way, valuing loyalty, deep connection, and enduring affection. This belief in love's permanence made him cherish relationships and approach them with sincerity and devotion.

Movies were more than just entertainment for Aryan; they were a mirror to his life. He found comfort and understanding in the stories on screen, using them as references to navigate his own experiences. Whether it was a tale of triumph over adversity or a romance that defied all odds, Aryan saw his life reflected in the characters and plots, drawing lessons and inspiration from them.

Like many young men, Aryan had a love for cars and bikes. They represented freedom and adventure, a dream of speeding down open roads and exploring new horizons. This passion was more than a mere fascination; it was a symbol of his aspirations and the journey he envisioned for himself.

Aryan's story was one of resilience, hope, and the pursuit of dreams against all odds. His love for music, despite the detour into medical school, highlighted his ability to adapt and find joy in unexpected places. His deep family bonds, especially with his brother, underscored his values of love and loyalty. His unique personality, straddling the line between introvert and extrovert, allowed him to connect with people on various levels. And his romantic ideals and love for adventure painted a picture of a young man who believed in the beauty and potential of life.

In Aryan, one could see a reflection of the struggles and hopes of many, a testament to the power of dreams, love, and resilience in shaping a meaningful life. His journey was a reminder that even when fate takes an unexpected turn, there is always a path to fulfillment and joy.

Introduction:- Suhani

Suhani was a girl of intriguing contrasts, her life a delicate balance between simplicity and ambition. Despite her quiet demeanor, she harbored dreams that reached for the sky, fueled by an intelligence that set her apart. She often found solace in solitude, preferring the quiet moments where she could indulge in deep thought and reflection. Her introverted nature provided her with a rich inner world, a sanctuary where she could retreat and rejuvenate.

Photography was one of Suhani's favorite hobbies. She loved capturing moments, particularly self-portraits that showcased her unique personality and style. Much like Geet from her favorite film "Jab We Met," she believed in being her own favorite person. Suhani's confidence was quiet yet unshakable, rooted in a deep appreciation of her own worth.

Though an introvert, Suhani's mind was a bustling metropolis of thoughts, constantly analyzing and contemplating every aspect of her life. This overthinking nature sometimes kept her awake at night, but it also fueled her creativity and problem-solving skills. Her intelligence was evident in the way she navigated challenges, always finding innovative solutions and new perspectives.

Family was at the core of Suhani's heart. She cherished her siblings, showering them with love and care. Her friends, too, held a special place in her life. Despite her preference for solitude, she nurtured her relationships with them, always ready to lend an ear or a helping hand. Her love for BTS was another testament to her passionate nature; their music and messages resonated deeply with her, providing both comfort and inspiration.

Suhani's favorite colors were purple and brown—purple for its association with creativity and spirituality, and brown for its warmth and reliability. Her culinary preferences were equally distinct. A non-vegetarian at heart, she relished the flavors of burgers and chili potatoes. Ice cream was her indulgence, with chocolate and rabdi kulfi as her top picks, each spoonful a celebration of life's simple pleasures.

Traveling was one of Suhani's greatest joys. She had a particular fondness for mountains over beaches, finding peace and inspiration in their majestic heights and serene landscapes. Road trips were her preferred mode of travel, blending her love for cars with her wanderlust. The act of driving through winding mountain roads was not just a journey but a meditative experience for her.

Regular visits to temples with her family were a grounding force in Suhani's life. These spiritual outings provided a sense of peace and connection, contrasting beautifully with her otherwise modern lifestyle. Badminton was another of her beloved activities, a sport where she could channel her energy and competitive spirit, balancing her introspective nature with physical vigor.

"Jab We Met," her favorite film, held a special place in Suhani's heart. She saw reflections of her own life in the story of Geet, the protagonist. Geet's optimism, independence, and ability to find joy in her own company were qualities Suhani admired and aspired to embody. The film was a reminder of the importance of self-love and staying true to oneself, themes that resonated deeply with her.

Suhani's life was a beautiful mosaic of passions, relationships, and dreams. Her love for solitude and introspection did not diminish her affection for her family and friends. Her intelligence and ambition were tempered by her appreciation for simple joys and spiritual grounding. In her, one could see a girl who embraced life with all its complexities, finding beauty and meaning in every moment.

Chapter 1: The Unforgettable First Day

My first day of college is something I'll probably never forget. It began with the chaos of a packed train ride. The early morning rush, the scramble for a seat, and the jostling crowds were a far cry from the tranquil mornings back home. As the train rattled towards the city, I stared out of the window, trying to gather my thoughts amidst the clamor. Dust from the roads swirled through the open windows, coating everything in a thin layer of grime. By the time I finally reached college, I was a mix of excitement and exhaustion.

With a deep breath, I stepped onto the campus, feeling a surge of positive energy. This was it, the place where I would achieve something big, learn new skills, and carve out my future. The buildings loomed large and imposing, each brick seeming to whisper promises of knowledge and opportunity. Yet, as I walked towards the main hall, I couldn't shake the feeling of uncertainty gnawing at the edges of my enthusiasm.

Inside, the atmosphere was a blend of nervous anticipation and burgeoning camaraderie. Students milled about, some already clustered in groups, chatting animatedly as if they had known each other for years. Others, like me, were still finding their footing, hovering awkwardly at the edges of conversations. I scanned the room, feeling a pang of envy for those who seemed to effortlessly strike up friendships.

Taking a seat in one of the rows, I observed the scene around me. Teachers began to file in, each one introducing themselves with a mix of authority and warmth. Their voices blended into a hum in my mind, the words becoming background noise as I grappled with my own thoughts. Was this really the right place for me? Doubt began to creep in, undermining the confidence I had felt that morning.

Suddenly, the door swung open, breaking my reverie. A girl hurried in, her red oversized T-shirt and blue jeans standing out against the sea of more conventional attire. Her simple ponytail swayed as she moved, a testament to her rushed entry. She glanced around, her eyes wide with a mix of apology and determination, before addressing the teacher, "May I come in, ma'am?"

The teacher nodded, a faint smile playing on her lips, and the girl quickly made her way to the second bench from the front. As she settled into her seat, I felt an inexplicable pull, a voice inside me whispering, "She's the one." It was as if the universe had paused for a moment to underline her presence in my life.

Throughout the rest of the session, I found it impossible to concentrate. My eyes kept drifting back to her, my thoughts circling around her like a moth to a flame. When the teacher started taking attendance, my heart skipped a beat as she called out the name, "Suhani." I repeated her name silently, savoring the sound of it, and from that moment on, I couldn't get it out of my head. It was as if it had become a part of me, a melody I couldn't stop humming.

I spent the entire day in a daze, my attention divided between the lectures and sneaking glances at Suhani. Her presence was a constant distraction, a beacon in the otherwise mundane proceedings of the day. I tried to rationalize my fascination, telling myself that it was just a fleeting crush, a product of first-day jitters. But deep down, I knew it was something more.

During a break, a guy from my village, Rohan, took the seat next to me. He was a familiar face in this sea of strangers, and I was grateful for his company. He nudged me with a grin, "Bro, how do you find the girl?"

Caught off guard, I shot him a glare, masking my embarrassment with irritation. "I came here to study, don't talk nonsense with me," I snapped, trying to shut down the conversation. But my heart was a traitor, beating out a different rhythm, echoing the thoughts I couldn't voice aloud. "Yeah, bro," it seemed to say, "she's going to be your sister-in-law no matter what."

Rohan laughed, clearly not buying my feigned disinterest. "Sure, sure," he said, giving me a knowing look. "But seriously, she's something, isn't she?"

I didn't respond, but my silence spoke volumes. I was torn between the desire to focus on my studies and the undeniable pull I felt towards Suhani. The rest of the day passed in a blur, punctuated by fleeting moments where our eyes would almost meet, and I would quickly look away, my heart racing.

That night, as I lay in bed, I replayed the events of the day in my mind. The excitement of stepping into a new chapter of my life, the overwhelming doubts, and above all, the unexpected encounter with Suhani. Her name was a constant refrain in my thoughts, a gentle reminder of the connection I had felt from the moment she walked into the room.

I realized that my first day of college was more than just an introduction to a new academic environment. It was a glimpse into the unpredictability of life, a reminder that sometimes, the most profound experiences come from the most unexpected places. As I drifted off to sleep, I knew that I was at the beginning of a journey, one that would be shaped by the people I met and the choices I made.

The next day, and the days that followed, I found myself looking forward to seeing Suhani, hoping for a chance to talk to her, to understand the connection I felt. My shyness was a hurdle, but the thought of her was a constant motivation, pushing me to step out of my comfort zone.

College, I realized, was not just about academics. It was about growing, learning, and discovering parts of myself that I never knew existed. And in that discovery, Suhani had become a pivotal part, a catalyst for change. As I embraced the journey ahead, I knew that my first day was just the beginning of a story yet to unfold.

Chapter 2: The Unspoken Infatuation

Aryan had never been able to muster the courage to speak to Suhani, despite his growing infatuation with her. Every day, he found himself admiring her from afar, his heart pounding with a mix of longing and nerves. The college campus buzzed with the excitement of new friendships, the formation of study groups, and the making of grand promises to stay connected throughout the course or even a lifetime. But Aryan knew better. He understood that nothing was truly permanent unless one made a conscious decision to make someone a lasting part of their life.

Aryan's days passed in a blur of lectures, assignments, and fleeting glimpses of Suhani. He noticed how effortlessly she moved through the campus, her presence radiating a quiet confidence that both intimidated and attracted him. Her laughter, the way she flipped her hair, and even her thoughtful expressions while reading a book—all these little details captivated him. His friends often spoke of their weekend plans, new crushes, and the latest gossip, but Aryan's thoughts always drifted back to Suhani. She was different. Special. And that made everything more complicated.

One crisp morning, as Aryan walked to college, his friend Rohan joined him, his usual playful demeanor evident. As they neared the college gates, Rohan nudged Aryan and asked, "So, what's the deal with Suhani? She seems nice."

Aryan's heart skipped a beat. He hadn't expected this. Caught off guard, he couldn't help but sing her praises, his words tumbling out faster than he could control. He spoke of her kindness, her intelligence, her beauty—every little detail he had noticed from afar. Rohan listened, a knowing smile playing on his lips.

"Whoa, slow down, lover boy!" Rohan teased, laughter in his voice. "I thought you were here to focus on studies, not get distracted by matters of the heart."

Aryan tried to backtrack, to downplay his words, but it was too late. Rohan had seen through him, and the teasing only grew. Despite Aryan's attempts to change the subject, Rohan remained suspicious, casting sly glances his way every now and then.

Days turned into weeks, and Aryan's resolve grew stronger. He decided he had to talk to Suhani, no matter what. Gathering all the courage he could, he approached her one afternoon. As he neared, his throat went dry, and his legs began to tremble. Anxiety washed over him, making it hard to breathe. She was sitting under a tree, engrossed in her books. He took a deep breath and stepped forward, but his voice betrayed him, and he couldn't utter a single word.

Dejected, Aryan walked home that evening, his mind a whirlwind of confusion. Why was it so hard to talk to her? He could converse easily with other girls, joke with them, and share stories, but with Suhani, it was different. Deep down, he knew the answer. The other girls were just that—girls. But Suhani was special, and that made him nervous, afraid of making a fool of himself in front of her.

Determined to break the ice, Aryan turned to his friend Vikas for advice. Vikas, always full of ideas, rattled off a long list of tips on how to approach girls. Aryan listened patiently, but most of the suggestions felt insincere, like they belonged in a movie rather than real life.

"Vikas, this all sounds too fake. I need something simple, subtle, and genuine," Aryan said, feeling frustrated.

Vikas paused, thinking. "Alright, how about this? Ask her for her notes. It's a great way to start a conversation, and it's perfectly normal."

Relieved, Aryan agreed. It was a straightforward plan, and it seemed authentic enough. He quickly found Suhani's number from their class group, though he doubted it was correct. Despite his doubts, he followed his heart's urging and sent her a text, asking for notes.

The next two hours felt like an eternity. Aryan's mind raced with possibilities, his phone never leaving his hand. When her reply finally came, he nearly dropped his phone in shock. She didn't have the notes he asked for, but she had replied. That simple message felt like a victory.

Overwhelmed with excitement, Aryan immediately called Vikas. "She replied! What do I do now?" he asked, barely able to contain his glee.

Vikas laughed, sharing in his friend's joy. "Calm down, buddy. Just keep it casual. Ask her where she's from, talk about common interests. Keep the conversation light and easy."

Aryan followed Vikas's advice, and their brief conversation flowed smoothly. For ten minutes, they exchanged small talk, and each message from Suhani made Aryan's heart soar. When the conversation ended, he couldn't stop smiling. He replayed those ten minutes in his mind for the next ten days, feeling like a fool but a happy one nonetheless.

That initial conversation, though brief, opened a door for Aryan. He realized that approaching Suhani wasn't an insurmountable task. Each day, he grew a bit bolder, their interactions becoming more frequent and relaxed.

Chapter 3: The First Phase of Overthinking

Many days passed, and I couldn't muster the courage to talk to Suhani. Each day was a cycle of hope and disappointment, where I found myself constantly on the brink of making a move, only to retreat back into my shell. The more I thought about approaching her, the more I convinced myself of my inadequacies. What if she found me boring? What if I stumbled over my words and made a fool of myself? My mind was a battlefield, and courage was the elusive prize.

Then, a new friend entered my life—Madhav. Contrary to his name, which conjured images of a calm and wise sage, Madhav looked like a bandit when I first met him. His rugged appearance, with a scruffy beard and a perpetual glint of mischief in his eyes, was intimidating at first. But beneath that rough exterior, there was a genuine warmth. He approached me one afternoon, flashed a crooked smile, and struck up a conversation. Gradually, we became friends, bonding over our shared classes and mutual love for cricket.

It was on a sunny Thursday that I finally gathered enough courage to talk to Suhani. I had spent countless nights rehearsing my lines in front of the mirror, analyzing every possible response she could give. The plan was simple: catch her in the library, where she often sat by the large window, lost in her books.

"Today, I will at least try," I told myself. But as they say, happiness can be fleeting.

That very morning, Madhav announced to our group, with the enthusiasm of a Bollywood hero, that he liked Suhani. He shared his feelings in such an open and carefree manner that it felt like he was narrating a scene from a film. My heart sank. Here I was, finally ready to step out of my comfort zone, only to find my new friend already sitting with her in the library, chatting away as if they had known each other forever. The first thought that crossed my mind was a mix of hurt and betrayal. Madhav was not just any guy; he was my friend. It was the first time I felt the sting of jealousy and the burden of overthinking.

At home, I tried to rationalize my feelings. "Maybe it's just an attraction," I told myself. "How can someone fall in love in such a short time?" I reassured myself that this was a fleeting phase, a crush that would soon dissipate. But deep down, I knew that my feelings for Suhani were more than just a passing fancy. It was my first phase of overthinking, where every interaction, every glance, was scrutinized and dissected.

The next day, Madhav called me to join him in the library. To my surprise, he introduced me to Suhani, pulling me into their conversation with ease. Suhani's smile was disarming, and her eyes held a warmth that made me feel at ease. We talked about our classes, our favorite books, and the upcoming college fest. For the first time, I felt a glimmer of hope.

The announcement of the college fest brought a new excitement to our otherwise mundane routine. The fest promised a series of events—singing, dancing, and various extracurricular activities. As a small-time bathroom singer, I decided to sign up for the singing competition. To my delight,

I noticed that Suhani and her close friend Apoorva had also signed up. Madhav, seeing this, decided to participate as well, his competitive spirit shining through.

From the next day, practice sessions began. It was a strange but wonderful routine—me, Suhani, Apoorva, and Madhav, meeting daily in the music room. It was during these practice sessions that I truly started talking to Suhani. Even if it was just for work, it felt like a victory. Suhani used to come daily in oversized T-shirts and jeans with sports shoes, her casual yet confident demeanor captivating me. And then she would sing. Her voice was magical, each note perfectly pitched, each word dripping with emotion. It felt like I was at a live Taylor Swift concert. Yet, I had to admit, her friend Apoorva sang even better, her voice a perfect blend of power and grace.

The daily "hi" and "bye" from Suhani became the highlights of my day. Even though I knew it was because of Madhav, it still hurt less than the silence. What could I do? I was entangled in the complex web of my emotions, trying to decipher whether this was infatuation, attraction, or something deeper. There are three stages of love: infatuation, attraction, and profound love. I kept trying to figure out which one it was.

As the fest approached, the intensity of our practices increased. The music room became our sanctuary, a place where we could escape the pressures of our academic lives and lose ourselves in the rhythm and melody of our songs. Suhani and Apoorva often led the sessions, their experience and talent guiding us through the intricacies of each piece. Madhav, with his boundless energy and infectious enthusiasm, kept our spirits high, making even the toughest rehearsals feel like fun.

One evening, after a particularly grueling practice, Suhani suggested we all take a break and grab some coffee. We walked to a nearby café, laughing and chatting about everything from our favorite movies to the latest college gossip. Sitting across from Suhani, I marveled at how effortlessly she commanded attention, her laughter like a melody that made everything else fade into the background.

Madhav, noticing my quiet admiration, nudged me playfully. "Aryan, you should tell Suhani about your singing skills. He's really good, you know," he said, winking at me.

I blushed, feeling the spotlight suddenly turn on me. Suhani turned her gaze towards me, her eyes sparkling with curiosity. "Really? I'd love to hear you sing, Aryan," she said, her voice sincere and encouraging.

I nodded, feeling a mix of pride and nervousness. "Maybe one day," I replied, my heart racing.

The days leading up to the fest were a whirlwind of activity. We spent countless hours perfecting our performances, supporting each other through moments of doubt and fatigue. It was during one of these late-night rehearsals that I found myself alone with Suhani. The others had left, leaving us to lock up the music room. As we gathered our things, Suhani turned to me, a thoughtful expression on her face.

"Aryan, can I ask you something?" she began, her voice soft.

"Of course," I replied, my heart pounding.

"Why do you sing?" she asked, her eyes searching mine.

The question caught me off guard. I had never really thought about it. "I guess... because it makes me feel alive," I said, realizing the truth of my words as I spoke them. "It's like an escape, a way to express what I can't put into words."

Suhani smiled, a knowing look in her eyes. "I feel the same way," she said. "Music has a way of touching the soul, doesn't it?"

In that moment, I felt a connection with Suhani that went beyond words, beyond the superficial interactions of our daily lives. It was a shared understanding, a recognition of a kindred spirit. And as we stood there, bathed in the soft glow of the dimming lights, I realized that my feelings for Suhani were not just infatuation or attraction. They were something deeper, something that I couldn't yet define but knew was significant.

The night of the fest arrived, bringing with it a mix of excitement and nervous energy. The auditorium was packed, the buzz of anticipation palpable. Backstage, we huddled together, offering words of encouragement and last-minute tips. Madhav, ever the showman, was in his element, his confidence infectious.

When it was our turn, we took the stage, the bright lights blinding for a moment before we adjusted. Suhani stepped forward, her voice filling the auditorium with a hauntingly beautiful rendition of our chosen song. Apoorva followed, her powerful vocals adding depth and emotion. And then it was my turn. I took a deep breath, stepping up to the microphone. As I began to sing, I felt the familiar rush of adrenaline, the music carrying me away.

The audience's applause was thunderous, their appreciation a validation of our hard work. We bowed, smiling at each other, the joy of the moment shared between us. As we left the stage, Suhani turned to me, her eyes shining with pride.

"You were amazing, Aryan," she said, her smile lighting up her face.

"Thanks," I replied, my heart soaring. "You too."

That night, as I lay in bed, replaying the events of the day, I felt a sense of contentment. The fest had been a success, our performances well-received. But more than that, it had brought me closer to Suhani, allowing me to see her not just as a crush but as a friend, a fellow artist. The lines between infatuation and love were still blurred, but I knew that whatever this was, it was worth exploring.

Over the next few weeks, our group continued to meet, the bonds forged during the fest growing stronger. We celebrated our successes, supported each other through challenges, and shared countless moments of laughter and camaraderie. Madhav and Suhani's friendship blossomed, their easy banter and shared jokes a testament to their growing connection. And while it still hurt to see them together, I found solace in my own growing friendship with Suhani

Chapter 4: The Cruel Irony of Love

It was a day I always knew would come. Somewhere deep in my heart, I had hoped it would either never arrive or that, by some stroke of fortune, I wouldn't notice it. Yet, here it was, staring me in the face with a cruel sense of inevitability. Suhani, the girl I had harbored a quiet crush on for as long as I could remember, had proposed to Madhav.

Madhav, my best friend.

Have you ever wondered how it feels when your first crush, someone who seems so perfect in your eyes, ends up falling for your best friend? Life has a peculiar way of adding layers to its script, ensuring that every twist brings with it a fresh wave of complexity. The day Madhav told me, his eyes shining with joy, my heart sank deeper than it ever had before.

"Hey man, guess what? Suhani proposed to me today!" he said, unable to contain his excitement.

I forced a smile, the words leaving my mouth feeling like shards of glass. "I'm happy for you, man. Congrats."

Inside, I was crumbling. How could I explain to Madhav that his happiness was inadvertently causing me pain? That behind my supportive facade, my heart was breaking into a thousand pieces? That evening, as I walked home, the weight of my emotions felt unbearable. I needed to talk to someone who could understand, someone who could help me carry this burden.

I called my elder brother, my life supporter, and my pillar of strength. "Bhai," I said, my voice trembling, "congrats, he got the girl." Tears streamed down my face as I spoke, my heartache evident in every word.

He noticed instantly. "Are you crazy? Don't ruin your focus and life over a girl. Just stay away from them," he said, a mix of frustration and concern coloring his tone.

How could I explain to him that it wasn't that simple? Even if I stayed away, I would still see them together, their happiness a constant reminder of what I had lost, or rather, what I had never had. How could I explain to my heart that it needed to let go?

Seeing Madhav and Suhani together became a daily trial. Their laughter, their shared moments, the way they held hands – it was all too much to bear. To protect myself, I began avoiding them. Whenever I saw them, I would walk the other way, not wanting to spoil our friendship with the bitterness of my unspoken feelings. Madhav was a good friend, and losing him over this seemed like an unbearable loss.

With time, acceptance started to set in. Reality, harsh as it was, had to be faced. I recalled the teachings of Lord Krishna in the Bhagavad Gita: we cannot force someone to love us back. These words became a mantra, a source of solace in my time of need. I started focusing on my career and honing my skills, channeling my pain into something productive.

In a strange way, I found happiness in this newfound focus. Perhaps it was for the best that I wasn't in a relationship. Maybe I wouldn't have been able to handle it anyway. Madhav was a nice guy; he would take good care of Suhani. With this thought, I found a semblance of peace.

But let me take you back to where it all began, so you can understand the depth of this journey and the lessons it has taught me.

MADHAV AND I WERE INSEPARABLE. We met in the first semester and quickly became the best of friends. Our bond was built on shared interests, mutual respect, and an unspoken understanding that we had each other's backs no matter what we always knowing that we could count on one another.

Suhani entered our lives.She was the new girl, and her presence brought a refreshing change to our otherwise predictable world. She was smart, funny, and incredibly kind – qualities that drew people to her effortlessly. I was no exception.

My feelings for Suhani developed gradually. It wasn't love at first sight, but a slow, steady realization that she was someone special. We became friends, and I cherished every moment we spent together. She had a way of making everything seem brighter, and I found myself looking forward to her company more and more.

Madhav, too, was drawn to her, but in a different way. While I harbored a silent affection, he was open and expressive. He made her laugh, shared his dreams with her, and supported her in ways that only a close friend could. It was clear to anyone who paid attention that he cared deeply for her.

For the longest time, I lived in a state of quiet turmoil. On one hand, I wanted to express my feelings to Suhani, to let her know how much she meant to me. On the other hand, I couldn't bear the thought of jeopardizing our friendship, or worse, causing a rift between Madhav and me.

So, I kept my feelings hidden, hoping that time would bring clarity.

AS WE PROGRESSED THROUGH , our lives became more intertwined. We participated in the same activities, studied for exams together, and celebrated each other's successes. Suhani's presence became an integral part of our daily routine, and with each passing day, my feelings for her grew stronger.

ONE EVENING, AS THE sun was setting, we found ourselves sitting by a lake, the water reflecting the vibrant colors of the sky. It was a serene moment, one that felt almost magical. Suhani was sitting next to me, her presence comforting and familiar.

"Isn't it beautiful?" she said, her voice soft.

"Yeah," I replied, looking at her instead of the view. "It really is."

We sat in silence for a while, just enjoying the moment. I wanted to tell her everything – how I felt, what she meant to me – but the words wouldn't come. Fear held me back, the fear of rejection, of losing the friendship we had built.

Just then, Madhav joined us, breaking the spell. "Hey, you two! Come on, we're starting a game of truth or dare. You can't miss it!" he called out, his enthusiasm infectious.

We got up and joined the group, but that evening by the lake stayed with me. It was a reminder of what could have been, a glimpse into a world where my feelings were known.

THE DAY SUHANI PROPOSED to Madhav was the day my world tilted on its axis. It was a bright, sunny day, the kind that seemed to mock my inner turmoil. Madhav had asked me to meet him at our favorite hangout spot after school. I had no idea what he was about to tell me.

When I arrived, he was already there, a wide grin on his face. "You won't believe what happened today," he said, barely able to contain his excitement.

"What?" I asked, genuinely curious.

"Suhani proposed to me!" he exclaimed, his eyes lighting up with joy.

For a moment, the world stopped. I felt like I had been punched in the gut, the air knocked out of me. But I managed to smile, to congratulate him, to play the part of the supportive friend.

Inside, I was a storm of emotions. I wanted to be happy for him, truly, but it was hard to ignore the pain in my heart. The girl I had quietly loved for so long had chosen my best friend. The irony was almost too much to bear.

IN THE DAYS THAT FOLLOWED, I struggled to come to terms with my feelings. Seeing Suhani and Madhav together was a constant reminder of what I had lost. They were happy, and as much as it hurt, I couldn't bring myself to wish them anything but the best.

Avoiding them became my coping mechanism. Whenever I saw them together, I would find an excuse to leave, to put some distance between us. I didn't want my presence to taint their happiness with my unspoken bitterness.

But life has a way of pushing us to face our demons. Despite my efforts to avoid them, there were moments when our paths crossed. Each encounter was a test of my resolve, a reminder of the need to accept reality and move forward.

ACCEPTANCE CAME SLOWLY. It wasn't a sudden revelation, but a gradual process of coming to terms with the situation. I realized that holding onto my feelings would only cause more pain, not just for me, but for everyone involved.

I turned to the teachings of Lord Krishna in the Bhagavad Gita, seeking solace in his wisdom. The idea that we cannot force someone to love us back resonated deeply. Love, true love, is not about possession or control. It's about respect, understanding, and the willingness to let go.

With this newfound perspective, I began to focus on myself. I threw myself into my studies and hobbies, channeling my energy into areas that would help me grow. It was a way to distract myself, but also a means to build a future that wasn't defined by unrequited love.

ONE EVENING, A FEW months after Suhani's proposal, I found myself sitting alone in a park. The sun was setting, casting a warm glow over the surroundings. It was a peaceful moment, one that offered a chance for reflection.

As I sat there, lost in thought, I realized................

Chapter 5: Shattered Illusions

Everything was going fine; I was slowly adapting to the environment because, of course, my parents had invested money and I needed to deliver results. The campus was a world unto itself, a microcosm of life bustling with ambition, laughter, and the occasional heartbreak. I had been fortunate enough to find a group of friends who made this new chapter of my life more bearable.

But perhaps my bad luck affected my friend too. It was library time, and I was walking towards the library holding a water bottle. Madhav, Suhani, Rohan, and Apoorva were sitting at one desk, and I was a bit away from them at another desk. The thing is, we went to the library only for fun and to enjoy the cool AC air. The library, with its vast collection of books and hushed ambiance, was our refuge from the outside chaos. We often pretended to study, but mostly, we were there to escape the heat and enjoy each other's company.

Suddenly, I noticed Suhani's expressions seemed different. Her usual vivacious demeanor was replaced by a tense, almost distant look. Madhav, who was usually the life of the group, also looked unusually serious. I started worrying. At that moment, I went over to ask them something trivial, maybe to break the ice, but they were deep in conversation, arguing about something. Initially, I thought it was just a normal argument, which happens to everyone, so I decided to leave it to Madhav to handle. If it escalated, I would step in; otherwise, I wouldn't, as it might send the wrong signals.

As the library session came to an end, we walked back to class in relative silence. A boring sociology lecture was going on, and we were dozing off, the professor's droning voice a lullaby to our tired minds. The classroom was stifling, and my mind kept wandering back to the library. I kept glancing at Suhani and Madhav, hoping to see some sign of reconciliation.

Then I noticed Madhav was missing. Suhani was in her place, but she seemed lost in thought, her gaze fixed on something beyond the walls of the classroom. A knot of dread tightened in my stomach. I started worrying about what might have happened. Unable to focus, I quietly slipped out of the classroom to look for him.

I ran through the corridors, my mind racing with possibilities. After what felt like an eternity, I found him sitting alone in a small space near the toilet, his shoulders slumped, his face a mask of dejection. Rohan followed me as well, concern etched on his face. As soon as I reached Madhav and asked him what happened, he started crying—a raw, gut-wrenching sob that tore at my heart. Trust me, at that time, I had no idea what to do—whether to calm him down or ask him what happened. I was confused myself.

Then he said, "Bro, we're separated now. She wants to end this." His voice was choked with emotion, each word a struggle. I was like, what the heck, bro? Why? He himself had no idea what was going on.

I had also talked to Suhani earlier, her words echoing in my mind like a haunting refrain. "Aryan, I tried to explain to him that we can be friends but not more than that due to some obvious reasons. Take care of Madhav, he is very good. The problem lies with me. Thank you, bye."

The rest of the day passed in a blur. Madhav's tears, Suhani's resigned expression, Rohan's quiet solidarity—all these images jostled for space in my mind. It felt like the ground had shifted beneath our feet, and we were struggling to find our balance.

THE AFTERMATH

That night, I lay in bed, staring at the ceiling, the events of the day replaying in my mind like a broken record. What had gone wrong between Madhav and Suhani? Their relationship had always seemed solid, an unspoken understanding between them that I envied. But perhaps there were cracks I hadn't noticed, fissures that had widened into chasms over time.

My thoughts drifted back to the beginning. We had all met during the first week of college, thrown together by the whims of fate and a shared schedule. Madhav was the heart of our group, his infectious energy drawing people to him like moths to a flame. Suhani, with her quiet grace and quick wit, complemented him perfectly. They were the golden couple, the ones everyone assumed would be together forever.

But forever is a long time, and assumptions can be dangerous.

I remembered the countless hours we had spent together—studying, laughing, dreaming about the future. Madhav and Suhani had always seemed so in sync, finishing each other's sentences, their hands intertwined like two pieces of a puzzle. It was hard to imagine one without the other.

And yet, here we were.

The next morning, I woke up with a sense of determination. Madhav needed me, and I wasn't going to let him down. I found him in the cafeteria, staring into his cup of coffee as if it held the answers to all his questions.

"Hey," I said, sliding into the seat opposite him.

He looked up, his eyes red-rimmed and weary. "Hey."

"How are you holding up?"

He shrugged. "I've been better."

We sat in silence for a while, the hum of conversations around us a soothing backdrop. Finally, I broke the silence. "Do you want to talk about it?"

He sighed, running a hand through his hair. "I don't even know where to start, Aryan. One moment, everything was fine, and the next, she tells me it's over. Just like that."

"Did she give you a reason?"

He shook his head. "Not really. She said something about being friends but nothing more. Said the problem was with her, not me. What does that even mean?"

"I don't know," I admitted. "But maybe it's not about you or her individually. Maybe it's just... circumstances."

He nodded slowly, his gaze distant. "Yeah, maybe."

Days turned into weeks, and the rift between Madhav and Suhani became a chasm. Our group dynamic shifted, the easy camaraderie replaced by an awkward tension. We tried to carry on as if nothing had changed, but the absence of their usual banter was a constant reminder of what had been lost.

Madhav threw himself into his studies, using academic success as a distraction from his emotional turmoil. I admired his resilience, but I also worried about him. He was like a candle burning at both ends, his light bright but fleeting.

Suhani, on the other hand, withdrew into herself. She still joined us for lunch and study sessions, but her presence was muted, her laughter less frequent. It was as if a part of her had been extinguished, and the void it left was palpable.

CONFRONTING THE PAIN

One evening, as we were walking back to the dorms, I finally gathered the courage to talk to Suhani. "Hey, can we talk?"

She looked at me, her eyes wary but curious. "Sure, Aryan. What's up?"

We found a quiet bench under a tree, the setting sun casting long shadows across the ground. "I just wanted to know... what happened between you and Madhav? I mean, you don't have to tell me if you don't want to, but I think understanding might help us all."

She sighed, her shoulders slumping. "It's complicated, Aryan. It's not that I don't care about him—I do, more than I can put into words. But sometimes, caring isn't enough. There are things in my life, in my past, that make it hard for me to commit to a relationship right now."

"DOES HE KNOW THAT?"

"I tried to explain, but I don't think he fully understands. It's not his fault, though. How could he? Some things are too personal, too painful to share."

I nodded, feeling a pang of sympathy. "I'm sorry, Suhani. I wish there was something I could do to help."

"Just be there for him," she said softly. "He needs his friends now more than ever."

NAVIGATING THE NEW Normal

As the weeks turned into months, we all adjusted to a new normal. Madhav and Suhani found a way to coexist, their interactions polite but distant. It was a fragile peace, but it held.

Madhav started to heal, bit by bit. He found solace in new hobbies—painting, hiking, anything that kept his mind and body occupied. I joined him whenever I could, our shared experiences strengthening our bond.

Suhani, too, seemed to find her footing. She opened up more, sharing glimpses of her past that helped us understand her better. She was stronger than I had realized, her resilience a quiet but formidable force.

And through it all, our group endured. We learned to navigate the complexities of friendship, love, and loss. We grew up, not in the way we had expected, but in the way we needed to.

Life has a way of throwing curveballs, of testing us in ways we never imagined. But it's in those moments of adversity that we discover who we truly are, and what we're capable of.

Chapter 6: The Flames of Confusion

They say if you want to confuse a simple man, light the flame of love in his heart; he will inevitably find himself ensnared in perplexity. Such was the case with Aryan, a young man whose heart had become a battleground of emotions. On one side was his good friend Madhav, steadfast and reliable, and on the other, the enchanting Suhani, the girl who had captured his heart at first sight. Despite this clear dichotomy, Aryan was still deeply confused, unable to decipher what his heart truly desired. He was engrossed in what he called his 'calculations,' trying to balance the scales of friendship and love.

From the beginning, Aryan had made numerous adjustments to honor the sacred bro code, the unwritten law of loyalty among male friends. It seemed like a small sacrifice at first, but the complexity grew over time. He relegated his interactions with Suhani to the online realm, maintaining a deliberate distance because he sensed that somewhere deep down, it was wrong to nurture feelings for his best friend's crush. Aryan had witnessed Madhav's tears for Suhani, the girl who had stirred his own emotions so profoundly, and this sight had compelled him to step back.

Life, they say, is all about the sacrifices one makes. Aryan had made his fair share, both for Madhav and himself. But just as every morning is followed by evening, an immutable law of nature, Aryan's life continued to move forward, albeit with a heavy heart. One fine day, Aryan found himself on a bus ride to college with Madhav, their usual routine. As the bus rumbled along the city's crowded streets, Aryan's attention was drawn to Madhav, who was deeply engrossed in a conversation with a girl from another college.

At first, Aryan dismissed it as casual chatter, the kind exchanged between acquaintances. However, the situation took a turn when Madhav went out of his way to escort the girl to her college. This unexpected gesture struck Aryan with a mix of anger and regret. The friend he considered his best friend had hidden such a significant part of his life from him. Aryan had distanced himself from Suhani, the girl he liked, to honor Madhav's feelings, only to discover this betrayal.

For several days, Aryan retreated into himself, his world narrowing to a tunnel of introspection and pain. He didn't talk to anyone, not even Suhani. She sensed his withdrawal and texted him, concerned, "Hey Aryan, is everything okay? You seem a bit off lately."

He responded with a curt, "Just busy with college stuff, nothing to worry about." He couldn't bring himself to tell her the truth, knowing it would only hurt her more.

Days turned into weeks, and the silence between them grew, a chasm filled with unspoken words and unresolved emotions. Aryan's trust in Madhav shattered completely when he uncovered a harsh truth: Madhav was a playboy, juggling multiple girls and playing with their emotions. The realization hit Aryan like a ton of bricks. The friend he had trusted implicitly, for whom he had sacrificed his own happiness, was not the person he thought he was.

One evening, as the sun dipped below the horizon, Aryan sat in his room, staring at the ceiling. The weight of his unexpressed feelings for Suhani bore down on him. He could no longer suppress them. With a surge of determination, he decided to take a bold step. He grabbed his phone and texted Suhani, "Hey Suhani, I've never said this before...but would you mind having a 'Chai Date' sort of thing with me? Because I need to tell you something.. and few things are better discussed over a coffee but if chai works for you I'm fine with that also

He waited, his heart pounding, hoping against hope for a positive response. But as fate would have it, Suhani declined.

Her refusal, though polite, was a blow to Aryan's fragile hope. It wasn't just the rejection; it was the realization that she might see him as just another online acquaintance. The situation grew awkward, and Aryan's worst fear came true. Suhani had sensed his feelings, and now she started to distance herself, slowly and steadily ghosting him from every social media platform.

In the days that followed, Aryan's life took on a gray hue. The vibrant colors of his emotions dulled, replaced by a persistent ache. He missed Suhani's presence in his digital world, the chats that had once brightened his days now conspicuously absent. He struggled to focus on his studies, his mind a whirlpool of regret and longing.

One evening, as he sat in his favorite café, staring blankly at his coffee, he overheard a conversation at the next table. Two girls were discussing relationships and the importance of communication. Their words struck a chord with him, and he realized he needed to confront his feelings head-on, not just for Suhani, but for himself.

Chapter 7: The Ghost of Love

"You know, it doesn't hurt when your favorite person ghosts you; it hurts when they socially ghost you, and you still have to face them every day"

This was the paradox that Aryan lived with. Suhani hadn't just disappeared from his digital life—no, that would have been bearable. Instead, she had vanished emotionally, leaving him adrift in a sea of confusion and longing, while still being physically present in his world.

Suhani ghosted Aryan, not on social media since they never really talked there, but in real life. Every day, he saw her, a vision of grace and laughter. He noticed everything—her laughter, her conversations, the way she moved, and despite his best efforts, he couldn't ignore her.

ARYAN'S DAYS WERE A monotonous loop, colored only by the brief moments when Suhani crossed his path. He would sit in the college cafeteria, sipping a lukewarm coffee, pretending to be absorbed in his medical textbooks. His friends chatted around him, their voices a distant hum, as his eyes tracked Suhani's every move.

Suhani had a daily habit of rushing to the washroom with her hair down as soon as she arrived at college. It was a ritual he had come to anticipate, a fleeting moment that made his heart skip a beat. He would see her running, her hair cascading behind her like a silken curtain. For a second, everything else faded away. His heart urged him, "Aryan, look. See how beautiful she is. How can you avoid her? Go and talk to her, ask her what went wrong. Is our friendship so fragile that it ended over a simple coffee date?" But, as usual, the courage never came.

The story continued with Suhani in detox mode, her presence a silent reminder of what once was. Aryan's mind raced with the same questions, over and over, like a broken record. What had he done? Was it something he said? Was it something he didn't say?

Aryan knew nothing more was going to happen. Maybe his role in her story was only meant to be this short. He clung to the hope that in another lifetime, he could prove himself and his love. As a medical student, he understood the complexities of the human mind, the tricks it played, the illusions it conjured. But despite this understanding, Suhani never left his thoughts. The same scenarios played out in his mind, offering a glimmer of hope that one day, Suhani would turn back and talk to him. On that day, he would tell her, "Yes, I'm madly in love with you." But guess what? By then, he had already fallen asleep, and morning had come, leaving the dream just a dream.

STAYING AWAY FROM SUHANI taught Aryan two things: manifestation and prayer. Once, Suhani herself had told him that if you pray sincerely, even God will listen; you just need a pure heart. This simple, naive boy, who knew nothing about worldly matters and only knew he was a Hindu when it came to religion, started believing in prayers and visiting temples. Wherever he went, he would say in his heart, "God, I don't want anything. Just keep the people I genuinely like happy, that's it." This prayer included everyone he cared about—his family, friends, and of course, Suhani.

It might sound a bit cringy, but it's the old-fashioned type of love from a silly boy. Aryan had many opportunities to talk to Suhani and break the ice in college, but as usual, something or the other would always come up.

One day, Aryan sat on a bench in the college courtyard, lost in thought. The sky was overcast, matching his somber mood. He remembered the first time he saw Suhani. It was during the freshman orientation, amidst the chaotic energy of new beginnings. She had been standing with a group of friends, laughing at something. Her laughter had caught his attention—a light, melodious sound that seemed to cut through the noise. He had been captivated instantly.

Chapter 8: Castles in the Air

Aryan was jolted out of his reverie by the sound of laughter. The college courtyard, usually a haven of tranquility for him, was now filled with the echoes of lively conversation. He looked up from his spot under the sprawling banyan tree and saw Suhani walking towards him, her friends in tow. His heart ached at the sight of her, the familiar pang of unrequited love tightening his chest, but he forced himself to look away, pretending to be engrossed in his notebook. As they passed by, he caught snippets of their conversation, and then, one of her friends mentioned a party that night.

"Aryan, you should come too," Apoorva, Suhani's friend, called out, noticing him sitting alone.

Aryan looked up, surprised and somewhat disoriented. "Me? I don't know..."

"Come on, it'll be fun," Apoorva insisted with a bright smile. "Suhani, tell him he should come."

Suhani glanced at him briefly, her expression unreadable. "Yeah, you should come, Aryan," she said softly, almost reluctantly.

He hesitated, unsure if he could handle being around her in such a social setting. But then, he remembered his promise to himself—to prove his love, no matter what. He had been dreaming of moments like these, building castles in the air during his idle moments. "Alright, I'll be there," he said finally, trying to sound more confident than he felt.

The rest of the day passed in a blur for Aryan. He couldn't focus on his lectures or his assignments. His mind kept drifting back to Suhani and the upcoming party. He wondered what he would say to her, how she would react. Every scenario he imagined seemed to play out like a scene from a movie, but reality, he knew, was often far less predictable.

THE PARTY

That evening, Aryan arrived at the party, feeling out of place and awkward. The music was loud, the lights dim, and the room was filled with people chatting and laughing. He scanned the room, looking for Suhani amidst the crowd. The thumping bass of the music seemed to echo his racing heartbeat. Finally, he spotted her near the bar, talking to a group of friends, her laughter like a melody he couldn't resist.

Summoning his courage, he weaved through the throng of partygoers, his palms sweaty and his mouth dry. "Suhani," he called out, his voice barely audible over the music.

She turned, a hint of surprise in her eyes. "Aryan, you made it," she said, her tone a mix of astonishment and curiosity.

"Yeah, I did," he replied, trying to sound casual and failing miserably. "Can we talk?"

Suhani hesitated, glancing at her friends, then back at Aryan. "Okay. Let's go outside," she said finally, leading the way to the garden behind the house.

They stepped out into the cool night air, the noise of the party fading behind them. Aryan took a deep breath, trying to calm his racing heart and gather his thoughts. The garden was bathed in the soft glow of fairy lights, casting a magical aura over the scene.

"Suhani, I don't know what happened between us," he began, his voice trembling slightly. "But I need to know. Did I do something wrong?"

She looked away, her expression pained. "No, Aryan. It's not you. It's me. I just... I got scared."

"Scared? Of what?" he asked, genuinely puzzled.

"Of getting too close," she admitted, her voice barely above a whisper. "I've been hurt before, Aryan. And I didn't want to get hurt again. So, I pushed you away."

Aryan felt a surge of hope at her words. "Suhani, I would never hurt you. I care about you. A lot," he said earnestly, reaching out to touch her hand.

She looked at him, her eyes searching his for sincerity. "I know. And that's what scares me," she confessed, her voice trembling with emotion.

He gently squeezed her hand, willing her to believe him. "You don't have to be scared. We can take things slow. Just... give us a chance," he pleaded, his heart laid bare before her.

Suhani hesitated, then squeezed his hand back, a small smile playing on her lips. "Okay. Let's try," she agreed, a glimmer of hope in her eyes.

REBUILDING TRUST

In the days that followed, Aryan and Suhani began to rebuild their friendship, piece by piece. They spent more time together, talking about everything and nothing, laughing at old jokes, and discovering new facets of each other. The walls Suhani had built around herself began to crumble, slowly but surely, as Aryan's patience and understanding melted away her fears.

One afternoon, they found themselves sitting on a bench in the college garden, the sun setting and casting a warm, golden glow over everything. The tranquility of the moment made Aryan feel closer to Suhani than ever before.

"Suhani, I need to tell you something," he said, his voice steady despite the butterflies in his stomach. "I'm in love with you. I have been for a long time."

Suhani looked at him, her eyes wide with surprise and something else—something that looked a lot like hope. "Aryan, I..."

"Wait," he interrupted gently, taking her hands in his. "Let me finish. I know you're scared. I know you've been hurt before. But I promise you, I will never hurt you. I love you, and I want to be with you. We can take it slow, at your pace. Just... give us a chance."

Tears welled up in Suhani's eyes as she looked at him, her heart torn between fear and the desire to believe him. "Aryan, I'm scared. But... I care about you too. More than I realized," she admitted, her voice breaking.

Aryan felt his heart swell with joy and relief. "We'll figure it out together. One step at a time," he promised, pulling her into a gentle embrace.

NEW BEGINNINGS

As the weeks turned into months, Aryan and Suhani's relationship blossomed, growing stronger with each passing day. They faced challenges and uncertainties, but they faced them together, their bond deepening with each shared moment and every heartfelt conversation.

They spent weekends exploring the city, discovering hidden cafes and beautiful parks. They studied together in the library, sometimes in comfortable silence, other times engaged in animated discussions about their favorite books and subjects. They supported each other through exams and projects, celebrating each victory and comforting each other in times of stress.

One particularly memorable day was when Aryan took Suhani to his favorite spot by the river, a place he had often retreated to when he needed to think or find solace. The view was breathtaking, with the river reflecting the colors of the sunset, creating a scene of serene beauty.

"Suhani, this place means a lot to me," Aryan said as they sat on the grassy bank, their hands entwined. "I come here when I need to clear my mind or just feel at peace. I wanted to share it with you."

Suhani smiled, touched by his gesture. "It's beautiful, Aryan. Thank you for bringing me here," she said, resting her head on his shoulder.

They sat there in silence, watching the sunset and feeling a sense of contentment and connection that words couldn't capture. It was in moments like these that Suhani realized just how deeply Aryan cared for her, and how much she had come to care for him in return.

FACING CHALLENGES

Of course, their journey wasn't without its hurdles. There were moments of doubt and insecurity, times when Suhani's fears resurfaced, threatening to pull her back into her shell. But Aryan's unwavering support and patience helped her navigate these turbulent emotions.

One evening, after a particularly difficult day, Suhani broke down, her fears and insecurities overwhelming her. "Aryan, I'm so scared," she admitted, her voice trembling. "What if I'm not good enough? What if I hurt you?"

Aryan cupped her face in his hands, looking into her tear-filled eyes with utmost sincerity. "Suhani, you are more than enough. And you won't hurt me. We're in this together, remember? I believe in us," he said firmly, his love and reassurance wrapping around her like a warm embrace.

Suhani took a deep breath, finding strength in his words and his unwavering gaze. "I believe in us too," she whispered, leaning into him for comfort.

AMID THE TRANQUIL LULL of early morning, a mother gently called out to her son, Aryan, urging him to wake from his slumber. "Aryan, my dear, rise and shine. Your dreams have lingered long enough; it's time to face the world and head to college."

In that tender moment, as the soft echoes of her voice dissolved, I found myself jolted from my own reverie. The dreamscape where I had wandered vanished like a wisp of smoke, leaving me in a stark, empty reality. All that I had conjured in my sleep—my castles in the air—had dissipated into the void.

Chapter 9: Unspoken Words

Slowly, days turned into weeks, and weeks into months. Despite all that time, Suhani never spoke to me. It wasn't for a lack of opportunity—there were plenty of chances to bridge the growing chasm between us. But each time, I failed to gather the courage. Every potential conversation was a battlefield in my mind, where hesitation won every time. On one hand, I convinced myself that she had no desire to talk to me. On the other, a nagging thought kept resurfacing: she could have at least told me why she stopped speaking to me. How could there be such enmity that she ceased communication without explanation?

Our relationship, once so easy and natural, had become a puzzle I couldn't solve. The void left by her silence gnawed at me daily, a constant reminder of my inaction. It seemed unfathomable that things could deteriorate to such an extent that she would sever all ties without a word. Each day, I replayed our last conversations, searching for a clue, an indication of where things had gone wrong, but none ever emerged.

Then one day, everything shifted. A friend of mine, Ravi, had a heated argument with a girl named Priya. Their loud, emotional confrontation had drawn a small crowd. I, being one of the few mutual friends who could mediate, stepped in to resolve their disagreement. It was an intense and delicate process, but eventually, we managed to find common ground. As I left the scene, feeling somewhat accomplished, the corridor's familiar surroundings felt unusually still. That's when I heard it—a voice from the past.

"Aryan," called a voice from behind. It was unmistakably Suhani's. My heart skipped a beat, but I kept walking, pretending I hadn't heard her. "Aryan, listen!" she called again, more insistent this time. I couldn't ignore her any longer. I stopped, turning slowly, my heart pounding in my chest.

Suhani approached me hesitantly. Her demeanor was softer than I had expected, her eyes reflecting a mixture of emotions. "Thank you," she said quietly, "for resolving their argument."

Her words, meant to be simple and straightforward, were a lifeline thrown into the churning sea of my thoughts. But instead of grabbing it, I did the unthinkable—I ignored her and walked into my classroom. The rudeness of my action hit me like a brick wall as soon as the door closed behind me. Everything had happened so fast that I barely had time to process it. It wasn't until I was seated, staring blankly at the blackboard, that the reality of what I had done sank in. Suhani had reached out, and I had pushed her away.

"Shit, what have I done?" I muttered under my breath. How could I have been so rude? So blind? My mind raced, replaying the encounter over and over. Guilt settled in, heavy and suffocating. The entire day, I could think of nothing else. Every scenario in my mind ended the same way—with me apologizing, seeking forgiveness for my behavior. But I never moved beyond the planning stage. The fear of her rejection, of her confirmed hatred, paralyzed me.

Days turned into weeks, then months. Each passing moment only deepened my regret. The calendar's dates changed, the seasons came and went. My beard grew thicker, the acne on my face marked the passage of time. Everything around me evolved, but my feelings for Suhani remained as steadfast as ever. I couldn't shake the guilt that clung to me, the nagging thought that maybe, just maybe, things could have been different if I had acted otherwise.

A year passed. The pain of lost opportunities never dulled. I carried my guilt like a constant companion. The weight of it, combined with my enduring feelings for Suhani, created a storm within me that refused to subside. I was haunted by "what ifs." What if I hadn't been so rude? What if I had asked her for a chai date one more time? Perhaps our story would have had a different ending.

Suhani's absence in my life left a void that nothing else could fill. I tried to immerse myself in studies, hobbies, and friends, but nothing could distract me from the ache in my heart. The world around me was in constant motion, but my inner turmoil kept me anchored to the past.

One evening, as the sun dipped below the horizon, casting long shadows across my room, I decided it was time to confront my feelings. I pulled out an old notebook and began to write. I poured my heart out onto the pages, recounting every memory, every emotion I had felt over the past year. It was cathartic, a release of the pent-up emotions that had threatened to overwhelm me. As I wrote, I began to see a pattern, a thread connecting each event, each feeling.

The notebook became my confidant, the pages absorbing my sorrow and my hopes. I wrote about the day I first met Suhani, the way her smile had lit up the room, the countless conversations we had shared. I documented the growing distance, the confusion, and the pain of her silence. And finally, I wrote about the day in the corridor, the regret that had consumed me since.

By the time I closed the notebook, I felt a sense of clarity I hadn't felt in a long time. I knew what I needed to do. The next day, with the notebook in hand, I went to the park where Suhani and I had spent many afternoons on chatting. I sat on myfavorite bench, the cool breeze rustling the leaves around me. Taking a deep breath, I began to read aloud from the notebook, imagining Suhani sitting next to me, listening.

It was a one-sided conversation, but it felt real. I read about my regrets, my feelings, and my hopes for the future. As I finished, I felt a weight lift off my shoulders. I knew that Suhani might never hear these words, but voicing them out loud was a step toward healing.

Weeks later, as I walked through the campus, I saw Suhani in the distance. Our eyes met for a brief moment, and I saw a flicker of recognition. My heart raced, but this time, I didn't look away. I gave her a small, hopeful smile. She hesitated for a moment, then returned the smile. It was a small gesture, but it spoke volumes.

From that day on, I promised myself that I would never let fear hold me back. Whether or not Suhani and I ever spoke again, I knew I had taken a step toward mending my own heart. And in that moment, I realized that sometimes, the greatest battles we fight are within ourselves. The courage to face our fears, to confront our regrets, and to seek forgiveness—these are the steps that lead to true healing.

As I continued on my journey, I carried the lessons I had learned close to my heart. The past year had been filled with pain and regret, but it had also taught me about resilience, hope, and the power of forgiveness. I knew that whatever the future held, I was ready to face it with an open heart and a renewed sense of purpose. And with each new day, I took one step closer to becoming the person I aspired to be—braver, kinder, and more willing to embrace the possibilities of life.

Chapter 10: The Closer It Gets

They say, "The more you try to run away from something, the closer it gets to you." Aryan had been living this paradox for months, trapped in a cycle of avoidance and regret. Every step he took to distance himself from Suhani seemed to draw her image closer to the forefront of his mind. It wasn't just her face that haunted him; it was the memory of her laughter, the way her eyes sparkled when she talked about something she loved, and the warmth of her presence. Aryan believed that avoiding her was the best way to move on, but deep down, he knew it was an illusion bound to break. Nothing is permanent in this world; if anything is permanent, it is only one thing: "prem"

It was January, the chill of winter still hanging in the air like a delicate mist over the city. The cold seeping through the windows of Aryan's small apartment seemed to mirror the frost on his heart. The day had been a blur of work and solitude, punctuated by the occasional text message or email. Aryan had been pushing through the days, burying himself in his college life and avoiding the friends and places that once meant so much to him. The ghosts of the past, particularly Suhani, lurked around every corner, in every quiet moment.

When he received the invitation to his cousin's marriage anniversary celebration, it came as both a relief and a distraction. The thought of an evening away from his own thoughts and the possibility of losing himself in the company of family was tempting. He almost didn't go, but the pull of familiarity and the desire for a temporary escape from his own misery drove him to accept the invitation.

The celebration was a vibrant tapestry of sound and color. Aryan entered the venue to find it filled with the laughter of children, the chatter of relatives, and the strains of old Bollywood music. The air was rich with the aroma of delicious food, a mixture of spices and sweetness that made his stomach rumble with anticipation.

Aryan's cousins greeted him with open arms, their faces bright with the joy of the occasion. He was swept into a whirlwind of hugs and playful banter. The evening was alive with energy, as they danced to the tunes of yesteryear, a nostalgic trip back to simpler times.

In the midst of the festivities, Aryan found himself smiling and laughing along with everyone else, if only to keep up appearances. The music was loud, the food was plentiful, and for a few hours, he allowed himself to be caught up in the moment. He chatted with his cousins, shared stories of past escapades, and even joined in the dancing, though his heart wasn't fully in it. His movements were mechanical, a performance of normalcy for the sake of others.

As the night deepened and the party began to wind down, Aryan found himself standing alone on the terrace, the cool breeze brushing against his cheeks. He looked out over the city, the lights twinkling like distant stars. The serene beauty of the scene contrasted starkly with the turmoil within him.

He leaned against the railing, staring into the darkness, and it was then that he heard the familiar melody of a song from the past. It was an old romantic track that had been one of Suhani's favorites. The melody drifted up from the dance floor below, a haunting reminder of moments shared, of times now lost. The song seemed to pull him back into the past, dragging with it the memories he had tried so hard to escape.

As the music played, Aryan closed his eyes, letting the melody wrap around him like a blanket. He was suddenly flooded with memories of Suhani—the way she would smile when she was excited, the sound of her laughter, the warmth of her handshake. Each memory was a vivid flash, a snapshot of a moment he had cherished but had now become a source of pain.

The song ended, but the memories lingered. Aryan felt the weight of his regret pressing down on him, each note of the song a reminder of how he had let go of something precious. He took a deep breath, trying to steady himself, and decided to find solace in the only comfort he knew: ice cream. He walked back into the house, heading straight for the kitchen.

In the quiet of the kitchen, Aryan reached for two bowls from the cupboard, filling them with his favorite ice cream. The cold sweetness of the dessert was a small comfort, a temporary balm for the ache in his heart. He scooped the creamy treat into the bowls, the simple act providing a moment of calm in the storm of his thoughts.

With the bowls in hand, he settled into a cozy corner of the living room, where he could see the festive chaos of the celebration in the distance. The room was adorned with fairy lights and decorated with the remnants of the party—empty glasses, half-eaten plates of food, and colorful streamers. It was a beautiful mess, a testament to the joy of the evening.

Sitting there, he began to eat his ice cream, each bite a small indulgence that gave him a momentary escape from his thoughts. As he ate, his mind wandered back to Suhani. He remembered the first time they had met, how her laughter had filled the room, and how her presence had been a light in his life. He remembered their conversations, the way she would talk about her dreams and aspirations, her passion for life.

He recalled a moment from their past, a simple exchange on a quiet evening. They had been chatting under the stars, talking about nothing and everything. Aryan had looked up at the moon and remarked, "Hey, the moon is beautiful today, isn't it?" Suhani had looked at his text with a puzzled expression, asking, "What?" He had brushed it off, saying, "Nothing, it was just a random thought," not wanting to risk their friendship by expressing more.

But now, months later, that memory was a sharp sting. He wished he had been braver, had said more. The regret gnawed at him, each bite of the ice cream unable to numb the pain.

He pulled out his phone, the idea of reaching out to Suhani forming in his mind. He hesitated, his fingers hovering over the screen. What would he say? How would she react? After a moment of indecision, he typed out a simple message: "Hey Suhani."

The seconds ticked by as he waited for her reply. He stared at the screen, his heart pounding with a mix of hope and dread. The minutes stretched into what felt like hours, his thoughts a jumble of what-ifs and regrets. Finally, after what seemed like an eternity, her reply came: "Hey Aryan, took you long enough to text me."

Her words were sharp, tinged with the hurt that he had caused her. Aryan took a deep breath, trying to steady himself. "She has every right to be angry," he thought. "I vanished without a word, left her to wonder what went wrong." He was prepared for a confrontation, for anger, for accusations.

The conversation began awkwardly, both of them treading carefully around the painful history between them. Aryan tried to explain himself, though he knew there were no easy answers. He told her about his struggles, his attempts to move on, but he knew these were mere excuses. The truth was that he had been afraid—afraid of the feelings he had for her, afraid of the vulnerability that came with love.

As they talked, Suhani brought up a detail that struck Aryan with the force of a revelation. She told him that it wasn't her but him who had removed her from his Instagram account. Aryan was stunned. "How did this even happen?" he wondered, searching for a plausible explanation. "Maybe it was a technical glitch," he thought, though the thought of this explanation felt hollow in the face of the truth.

He couldn't deny that he had acted thoughtlessly. The way he had withdrawn from her life without explanation had been a mistake, a lapse in judgment that had caused her pain. His heart ached as she recounted moments he had forgotten or tried to bury. She brought up a time when they had been chatting late at night, and he had mentioned the beauty of the moon. She had been struggling with her own feelings of numbness, and his casual comment had been a fleeting but significant moment for her.

Suhani had remembered that night vividly. "Dude, I was actually feeling numb when you said that damned moon thing," she told him, her voice tinged with the sadness of the past. "But guess what, within a week, you just vanished from my life."

Her words hit him like a physical blow. Aryan realized, with a clarity that was almost painful, how deeply he had hurt her. He saw now how his actions had been a source of confusion and heartache for her. The realization was overwhelming, and he struggled to find the words to express his remorse.

"I'm so sorry, Suhani," he said, his voice barely above a whisper. "I never meant to hurt you." The apology was sincere, but it felt like a small gesture compared to the depth of the pain he had caused. He wanted to make things right, but he didn't know how.

"What do I need to do to make it up?" he asked, his heart heavy with regret.

Suhani's response was calm but firm. She spoke about the importance of communication, about how their failure to talk openly had led to their estrangement. Her words were a mix of sadness and resignation, but there was also a hint of hope. She made it clear that their lack of communication had been a significant factor in their separation.

Chapter 11: A Simple, Subtle Date

Manish Behl once said in one of his movies that a boy and a girl can never be friends, which might be somewhat true. But someone else also said that if the same boy and girl go out to eat somewhere, it should be called a simple, subtle date, not just a get-together.It was a pleasant and fresh morning for Aryan, full of hope. As soon as he woke up, he ran straight to his village to get his elder uncle's (tauji's) bike—a majestic Royal Enfield. Now, it's a simple fact that a lazy boy who finds it tough to wake up early would not do so just to go to college, especially not for a bike. Yes, the reason could only be one person: Suhani.

The Night Before

Aryan had tossed and turned in his bed, unable to sleep. The thought of asking Suhani out had plagued him for weeks. His friends had given him endless advice, most of it conflicting. Finally, he decided to go with his gut and ask her out for tea. After all, it was just tea, right? But in his heart, he knew it was more than that.He picked up his phone and opened the chat with Suhani. His fingers hovered over the keyboard, unsure of what to say. Should he be casual or straightforward? Should he hint at his feelings or keep it light? He took a deep breath and typed, "Hey Suhani, would you like to have tea with me tomorrow?"He stared at the message, debating whether to send it. Before he could second-guess himself, he pressed send. The message was out there, and there was no turning back. Seconds felt like hours as he waited for her response. Finally, the typing indicator appeared, and his heart raced."Yes, okay," she replied.Aryan couldn't believe it. She had said yes! He jumped out of bed and did a little victory dance. Tomorrow was going to be the best day ever.

The Morning of the Date

Aryan woke up at the crack of dawn, something he never did willingly. The excitement of the day ahead had him wide awake. He quickly got dressed and ran to his village to borrow his tauji's Royal Enfield. The bike was a beauty, and Aryan knew it would impress Suhani.After a bit of scolding from his tauji for waking him up so early, Aryan was on his way. The morning air was crisp, and the sky was painted with hues of pink and orange. Aryan felt a sense of exhilaration as he rode the bike, the wind blowing through his hair. He plugged in his earphones and let the music carry him away. Today was going to be perfect.Meeting SuhaniUpon reaching college, Aryan's eyes scanned the crowd, looking for Suhani. He was early, which was a rare occurrence for him. He paced nervously, checking his watch every few seconds. Finally, he saw her walking towards the classroom. She looked stunning, her hair loose and flowing. Aryan's heart skipped a beat.Suhani placed her bag in the classroom and rushed to the washroom to fix her hair. Aryan couldn't help but smile. He wished he could tell her to leave her hair loose, as it made her look even more beautiful.When Suhani finally emerged, Aryan greeted her with a handshake. Her touch was soft, and Aryan felt a jolt of electricity run through him. He thought to himself that he could die happily now, as this was all he wanted from life.The LecturesThe lectures were a blur for Aryan. His mind was elsewhere, thinking about the date. Pharmacology and pathology felt like unnecessary obstacles in his path to happiness. Everyone around him was focused on ranks and grades, but Aryan knew that life was about more than that. True life was based on love, not ranks.Unlike many who lose focus due to love, Aryan remembered his priorities. He was in college not just for a degree, but for skills. He had unique plans for his life, which he would achieve with hard work and a bit of luck.

The Date

After the lectures, Aryan asked Suhani if they could leave. She made a weird face, but Aryan reminded her that she had agreed to go out with him. She asked where they should go, and Aryan suggested a newly opened café. She agreed to meet him outside the college.Aryan approached her on his bullet bike, and she was in shock, covering her face but her eyes revealing everything. They talked randomly about college stuff, breaking the initial awkward silence.Upon reaching the destination, Aryan realized the café wasn't there. Awkwardly, he asked Suhani where they should go, and she suggested a nearby famous restaurant. Aryan agreed and followed Suhani to a table inside. He realized that modern dating etiquette, like pulling a chair for the girl, didn't apply here as Suhani viewed this as just a get-together.Aryan knew that if he tried anything fancy, Suhani would probably hit him with whatever was on the side table and leave. So he quietly sat down."Chhole bhature and two lassis, please," Suhani ordered with confidence. It was one of her favorites, and Aryan could tell she was at ease.The best part was that the usual distance between them was now just a table. Suhani was talking while Aryan noticed her eyes,those eyes man. Well at first glance her eyes are brown but when the light hits them they change to amber and if you look really closely around the iris, the colour is pure honey but when you look into the sun,they almost look green that's my favourite and yeah,a small but cute mole on her right side of the face, falling for her again with every bite she took. Her eyes up close brought shayari to his mind, but he decided to write it in his diary later.As they ate, Suhani talked about her childhood, her family, and her dreams. Aryan listened intently, captivated by her voice and her stories. She spoke with passion about becoming a wise person and helping people. Aryan admired her dedication and determination."What about you, Aryan? What are your dreams?" Suhani asked, looking at him with curious eyes.Aryan hesitated for a moment. "I want to become a musician," he said. "I know it's going to be tough, but I believe I can do it. I want to make a difference, like you."Suhani smiled, and Aryan felt his heart melt. "That's wonderful," she said. "I believe in you."After eating, they left because Suhani had to reach home in 45 minutes. Aryan didn't want to go back, but she had to. She asked if he would drop her home, and he jokingly said he would follow her to hell if needed, but she didn't hear him.After some chit-chat, they headed to her home, where Aryan dropped her off. As she was leaving, he asked about their unfinished tea, and she offered to make tea at her home. Aryan, wanting to say yes, decided against it and said no.Watching her leave, he wished he had a time machine to freeze this moment forever. Aryan rode home listening to romantic songs, thanking Suhani for the day as soon as he got back.

Flashbacks and Musings

As Aryan lay in bed that night, he replayed the day's events in his mind. Every smile, every word, every glance from Suhani was etched into his memory. He pulled out his diary and began to write:"Her eyes are like the stars, guiding me through the darkest nights. Her smile is the sunrise, bringing warmth and light to my world. Today was more than a date; it was a glimpse into a future filled with love and hope."He closed the diary and placed it under his pillow. Aryan knew that life was unpredictable, but for now, he was content. He had taken a step towards something beautiful, and no matter what the future held, this day would always be special.

Suhani's Perspective

Meanwhile, Suhani sat in her room, reflecting on the day. She hadn't expected to enjoy Aryan's company so much. He was different from the other boys—genuine, kind, and passionate about his dreams.She thought about how nervous he had seemed at the restaurant, how his eyes had lit up when he talked about his aspirations. Suhani smiled to herself, feeling a warmth spread through her chest. Maybe there was something more to this get-together than she had initially thought.

The Beginning of Something New

The next day at college, things felt different. Aryan and Suhani shared a silent understanding, a connection that hadn't been there before. They greeted each other with smiles that held secrets only they knew.As days turned into weeks, Aryan and Suhani's friendship deepened. They spent more time together, studying, laughing, and sharing their hopes and fears. Aryan's feelings for Suhani grew stronger, and he knew that he wanted to be more than just friends with her.

Chapter 12: The Complexity of Friendship

Before the Fall

Someone once said that before everything gets better, it completely falls apart, but the guarantee of it getting better is absolute. This sentiment resonated deeply with Aryan as he navigated the complex relationship he shared with Suhani. They were two souls intertwined in a web of emotions, yet striving to keep their bond purely platonic. The journey from acquaintances to friends, and potentially something more, was fraught with challenges, uncertainties, and moments of introspection.

Aryan had always believed in the importance of friendship. Growing up, he had seen many relationships around him deteriorate because of misunderstandings and unexpressed feelings. His own parents had a tumultuous relationship that eventually ended in a painful divorce. This experience had shaped Aryan's views on relationships, making him wary of crossing the delicate line between friendship and love.

The Bonding Begins

Aryan and Suhani had started talking more frequently, each conversation adding another layer to their burgeoning friendship. They were becoming good friends. Yes, friends. Aryan cherished these interactions, as did Suhani, though she might not have expressed it as openly. Their conversations had a natural flow, filled with shared interests and mutual respect.

In the modern world, where relationships often blur the lines between friendship and love, Aryan made a conscious decision. Every guy always chooses friendship over love, he believed, because he knows that love is passionate, but friendship is peaceful. Aryan did the same. He valued the tranquility of their connection, understanding that love could bring about a storm of emotions he wasn't ready to face.

Suhani, on the other hand, had her own reasons for valuing their friendship. She had always struggled with social anxiety, finding it difficult to connect with people on a deeper level. Aryan was one of the few people who made her feel comfortable and understood. Their friendship provided her with a sense of security that she cherished deeply.

The Complexity of Communication

They started talking, even if it was just through text, but there was peace, and everything seemed to be going well. Their conversations ranged from mundane daily activities to deeper philosophical discussions. Each text was a thread weaving them closer together, yet maintaining the boundaries they had mutually agreed upon.

Aryan knew that Suhani was a bit anxious about talking in person. This was something he had sensed early on, in the way she sometimes hesitated before speaking, the slight tremor in her voice during their rare phone calls, and her preference for texting over face-to-face interactions. This suspicion was confirmed when she herself said, "I feel social anxiety when talking in person, so I'd never initiate a conversation."

From that point, Aryan started searching for ways to help reduce Suhani's social anxiety. He read articles, watched videos, and even spoke to friends who had similar experiences. His intentions were genuine; he wanted to make Suhani feel comfortable and secure, hoping that this would strengthen their friendship

Final Chapter: Crossed Paths

The life of a medical student is already a roller-coaster ride, but when emotions get tangled in the web of academic struggles, it becomes even more complex. Aryan and Suhani had started as casual acquaintances, their interactions limited to shared classes and occasional outings. The world of online classes was impersonal, but it had its advantages; it masked the vulnerabilities and awkwardness of in-person interactions. They had navigated this terrain well, forming a bond that felt promising and genuine.

As the days progressed, their relationship blossomed into a cherished friendship. They shared laughter over ice cream, discussed medical cases with fervor, and enjoyed the simplicity of each other's company. It was a beautiful phase where everything seemed perfect. Aryan cherished these moments, finding solace in their companionship amidst the demanding schedule of medical school.

Then came the clinical postings, a reality check that disrupted their serene bubble. Aryan was assigned to a different hospital from Suhani. The initial shock was hard to process. He had gotten used to seeing her every day, and now, the thought of not having her around was daunting. Determined to keep their connection alive, they made a pact. Aryan would sneak out during his breaks, pick her up from her hospital, and they would walk to her home together. Those brief moments of togetherness were a lifeline for Aryan. Just five minutes with her could rejuvenate him, giving him the strength to face the next 24 hours.

However, life had other plans. As days turned into weeks, Aryan sensed a shift in Suhani's behavior. She became distant, her responses to his messages delayed, her enthusiasm waning. He tried to brush off his suspicions, attributing them to the stress of their clinical rotations. But the nagging feeling wouldn't go away. One scorching afternoon, while attending to an irritable patient, Aryan's mind spiraled into a whirlpool of doubts and questions. What was wrong with Suhani? Why was she pulling away? The urge to confront her was overwhelming, but he held back, fearing he might push her further away.

In a moment of clarity, he decided to broach the topic casually during their next walk. He asked if everything was okay, hoping for a simple reassurance. Her response was nonchalant, "Everything is fine." But Aryan wasn't convinced. He couldn't shake off the feeling that something was amiss. He wanted to lay his heart bare, to tell her how much she meant to him

and how her aloofness was tearing him apart. But he held back, fearing it might come off as

desperation.

Days turned into weeks, and Aryan's frustration grew. He couldn't concentrate on his studies; his

mind was constantly preoccupied with thoughts of Suhani. One evening, he decided to confront

her directly. He poured out his heart, expressing his confusion and hurt. Her response was cold

and detached. "I don't care anymore about what anyone thinks of me. But let me tell you, I'vealways been like this. I can't hang out with someone daily. I can't talk on the phone for 24 hours for you or for me. Our definitions of friendship are different."

Her words hit him like a punch to the gut. He realized that perhaps he had been too intense, too demanding in his expectations. Suhani's perspective on friendship was different from his, and he had failed to see that. The argument that followed was brief but painful. The next day, Aryan tried to apologize, hoping to mend the rift. But Suhani remained distant, her demeanor indicating that she had moved on.

Aryan was left to grapple with his emotions. He had always prided himself on being perceptive, on recognizing his mistakes quickly. But this time, it felt different. The chasm between them seemed insurmountable. He made a few more attempts to reach out to her, but the silence from her end was deafening. Eventually, he realized that it was time to let go. Holding on would only cause more pain for both of them.

He decided to focus.

Aryan had thought their bond was unbreakable. But life has a way of surprising us, often in the most unexpected ways.The last conversation they had played over in his mind like a broken record. Suhani's voice had been calm but resolute, a stark contrast to the whirlwind of emotions inside Aryan."It would be easier to move on if we stayed out of sight," she had said, her eyes avoiding his. Aryan had nodded, unable to find the right words. How could he argue with her when all he wanted was for her to be happy?Days turned into weeks, and weeks into months. Aryan tried to fill the void with work, hobbies, and even new friendships. But nothing seemed to fill the gap Suhani had left behind. He often found himself reaching for his phone to share a funny meme or a random thought, only to remember that Suhani wasn't a part of his daily life anymore.His friends tried to console him, suggesting that he should move on, find someone new, or at least distract himself. But Aryan's heart wasn't ready to let go. He clung to the memories, the shared moments, the unspoken understanding they had always had.One evening, as he walked through the park where they used to meet, Aryan's thoughts drifted to what Suhani had said. "It would be easier to move on if we stayed out of sight." He pondered over it, trying to make sense of her perspective. For Suhani, out of sight might indeed be out of mind. She had always been pragmatic, knowing when to hold on and when to let go.But Aryan was different. His heart was stubborn, clinging to the hope that maybe, just maybe, they would find their way back to each other. He believed that true love wasn't something that faded in just six months. It was something that stayed, even if buried deep within.He remembered a conversation he had with his grandfather years ago. "Love isn't about possession, Aryan. It's about appreciation. Sometimes, loving someone means letting them go, even if it breaks your heart."Aryan sighed, sitting on the bench they had often shared. He realized that holding on to Suhani wasn't fair to either of them. She deserved to be happy, even if it meant without him. And maybe, he deserved to find his own happiness too.He pulled out his phone and scrolled through old messages and photos, a bittersweet smile playing on his lips. He would always cherish those moments, but it was time to create new ones. For both of their sakes.As the sun set, casting a golden hue over the park, Aryan made a silent promise to himself. He would let go, not because he wanted to, but because he had to. Suhani's happiness was worth it. And maybe, in the process, he would find his own path to healing.Life moved on, as it always does. Aryan found solace in new experiences, new connections. The pain of losing Suhani never truly went away, but it became a part of him, shaping him into a stronger, more empathetic person. He understood now that love wasn't just about holding on. Sometimes, the greatest act of love was knowing when to let go.And so, Aryan continued his journey, carrying the memories of Suhani in his heart, but also making room for new ones. He learned that love, in all its forms, was a powerful force, capable of breaking us and healing us, often at the same time. And in that, he found a sense of peace, knowing that whatever the future held, he would face it with an open heart and an unwavering spirit.

IN THE END, ARYAN WROTE a heartfelt note for Suhani, one he never mustered the courage to give her. Fearing he might disturb her once more, he chose to keep it to himself. It was his final, unspoken message to her.

Last Note: FROM HIM TO HER

OYE SUN,

How are you? I hope you're fine.

I've gathered some courage and written something for you today. I don't know if it's right or not, but here it is, without any expectations or hoping for anything in return. First of all, I really miss you. I know I'm very stupid, and I know I made mistakes. I'm aware of all of them. You're right when you say there's nothing left to save between us. But for me, whatever it is, however it is, it's a lot. Trust me, every moment I spent with you is something I'll keep in a safe box in my heart. People tell me to move on, but I can't. Actually, I don't want to. I haven't done much in my life bas 2 gaane gaaye hai aur ishq karaa hai with a girl from another planet. And trust me, you're the best thing that has ever happened to me. I thank life daily for that, but at the same time, I feel guilt. When I sit quietly and analyze this whole process, I come to one conclusion: yes, I made a lot of mistakes. But one thing has grown like a disciplined student throughout this process, and that is my feelings for you. Don't worry, I'm not expecting anything in return, so stay cool. I've analyzed myself a lot, and you know I have a disorder. Maybe that's why I can't stay angry with anyone for long. When I get angry, I end up hurting myself. Yes, it's true. You know how big of a fool I am. This fool has written something colorful for you. If you look at it, it'll be a favor, but before that, tell me, do you remember?

I always keep asking some questions, right? Today, for the last time, let me ask:

1. You said if I disappeared, you'd come looking for me like Rancho. Will you?

2. You once talked about going to Bet Dwarka. Will you come with me?

. 3. You talked about a lifetime subscription. Will you subscribe?

4. We planned to rob a bank together. The plan is ready. Will you join me?

5. You said if we ever felt stressed about the future, we'd sit and cry together. Now I'm stressed about your absence. Will you sit with me?

6.Our tea date is still pending, would you go with me to complete it?

Just because we don't talk anymore doesn't mean I've forgotten about you. It doesn't mean I no longer care, because the truth is, I still do. I often find myself checking up on you, wondering how you're doing. All I want is to hear your voice and talk to you, but every time I feel the urge to reach out, it hits me that we are strangers now. Even though everything has changed, I want you to know that in another universe, I'm still here for you. I'd still lend you my shoulder and my ear, no matter the time or what I'm doing, because I often wish you were talking to me.

There will always be a place in my heart that hurts whenever I think of you. A part of me will always care for you. And maybe in another universe, you'll be mine.

Maybe in another universe, we found each other at the right time, in the right place, with the right situation, and with hearts ready to intertwine. In that universe, our paths crossed with the precision of a perfect symphony, and every note played in harmony. We shared moments of pure joy, unburdened by the doubts and fears that cloud our reality. In that world, we laughed more, loved more, and held each other through every storm. Maybe in that universe, we are living the story I always dreamed of, the one that feels just out of reach in this one. And now, I ask myself a question: "Why not in this universe?"

And maybe, just maybe, the longing I feel in this universe is a whisper from that parallel existence, a reminder that somewhere, in some form, my love is as timeless and true as I always believed it could be.

As Ted Mosby once said, "If you're looking for the word that means caring for someone beyond all rationality and wanting them to have everything they want no matter how much it destroys you, it's love. And when you love someone, you just don't stop. Ever. Even when people roll their eyes, or call you crazy, even then, especially then."

Listen to me, I didn't fall in love with you because I was lost or broken or needed to be fixed. I fell in love with you because after getting to know you and who you are, I wanted to make you a permanent part of my world. The places and scenery may change, but whether it is for 5 minutes or 50 years, I would have just been happy to have you in it.

I know I should've stopped then...

But your smile just pulled me closer...

I know I shouldn't have been like this...

But your voice did call me to you...

I know we weren't meant to be in this journey...

But my mind was blind and my heart was beating for you...

I know I should've stayed your friend...

But my heart was asking to make you my life....

I know I am not perfect for you anyhow...

But your perfection showed me a better life...

I know I will never forget you for this life...

But I wish if I could wait for a lifetime to be with you...

I know I get angry, and my words might hurt you... But I can't stay alive when your face goes upset...

I know, I know that I love you so much...

But tell me, please, how not to...

I know, I know that I can't forget you... But do hurt me enough to unlove you this time...

Alas, I forgot how to not love you... For I see myself in your eyes this day, this night...

Can I not be your infinity to calm my pounding heart...

Leaving you for your happiness was my last gift to you, but trust me, I can wait. I will wait until the timing is right, when all the stars are aligned, and you are ready for this love of mine. Take your time, clear what is on your mind because, to me, you are worth the fight.

I fell in love with you because it felt so right, and you're the person who's worth getting hurt for. As Patrick said, "Everyone is going to hurt you... you just have to find one worth suffering for." You're worth suffering for.

No, don't feel numb. You are a strong and independent woman. And yes, I remember, I'm not going to protect you because you're a woman; I'm going to protect you because you're my woman.

No, Suhani, if you're feeling sad or like crying, don't cry. Instead, go to your 10th floor ki balcony aur ek sawaal hai jo puxna padega uska jawaab do..

THE MOON IS BEAUTIFUL, ISN'T IT?

AFTER ALL THIS TIME,they asked
   ALWAYS,the sentiment echoed softly
   BECAUSE IT'S NOT OVER UNTIL IT'S OVER